The
GRAND CANYON
Burros That Broke

by
Steve Brezenoff

illustrated by
Marcos Calo

Field Trip Mysteries are published by Stone Arch Books
A Capstone Imprint
1710 Roe Crest Drive
North Mankato, Minnesota 56003
www.capstonepub.com

JUL 2012

Library of Congress Cataloging-in-Publication Data
Brezenoff, Steven.
The Grand Canyon burros that broke / by Steve Brezenoff ;
illustrated by Marcos Calo.
p. cm. -- (Field trip mysteries)
ISBN 978-1-4342-3788-0 (library binding) -- ISBN 978-1-4342-
4198-6 (pbk.)
1. School field trips--Juvenile fiction. 2. Donkeys--Juvenile
fiction. 3. Grand Canyon National Park (Ariz.)--Juvenile
fiction. [1. School field trips--Fiction. 2. Donkeys--Fiction.
3. Animals--Fiction. 4. Grand Canyon National Park (Ariz.)--
Fiction. 5. Mystery and detective stories.] I. Calo, Marcos,
ill. II. Title. III. Series: Brezenoff, Steven. Field trip
mysteries.

23.99

Graphic Designer: Kay Fraser

Summary: Edward "Egg" Garrison and his friends
in the Art Club are on a trip to the Grand
Canyon when three riding burros mysteriously
disappear.

Printed in the United States of America in
Stevens Point, Wisconsin.
032012   006678WZF12

TABLE OF CONTENTS

Edward G. Garrison

A.K.A: Egg

D.O.B: May 14th

POSITION: 6th Grade

This can't be correct. Please confirm.

INTERESTS:

Photography, field trips

KNOWN ASSOCIATES:

Archer, Samantha; Duran, Catalina; and Shoo, James.

NOTES:

Ms. Stanwyck encourages Edward's passion for photography, but some teachers complain of the frequent use of the flash.

Is photography allowed in school? I will look into this.

AN ARTIST'S DREAM

The Art Club trip over spring break was a photographer's dream. Of course, it was also a painter's, sketcher's, and sculptor's dream. We were all excited to visit the Grand Canyon.

But I think I was the only one taking photos before our plane even landed at the airport in Flagstaff, Arizona.

"You better put that camera away," my friend Gum said. He sat next to me on the flight. Gum isn't his real name, just like Egg isn't my real name. His real name is James Shoo. But that's another story.

"Why?" I said. I clicked photo after photo, with the camera right up against the window.

I heard a grown-up clear his throat, so I looked up. The flight attendant was standing at our row with his arms crossed. He didn't look happy. "All electronic equipment," he said slowly, "must be put away. Now!"

Gum and I flinched. "Sorry," I said. "I guess I didn't hear the captain's announcement."

"He said it four times!" the attendant said. Then he stomped off.

I put my camera away.

"I tried to warn you," Gum said. He shrugged and put a piece of gum in his mouth. It smelled like peanut butter and jelly flavor.

I turned my head to peek through our seats to the row behind us. Cat and Sam, our two best friends, peeked back.

"I guess we're about to land," I said.

"Yup," Cat said, smiling. "I can't wait to start a new painting."

I smiled back, and then settled in my seat.

"I'll you one thing," Gum said, chewing happily on his gum. "I'm glad this trip is just for the Art Club."

"Why's that?" I asked.

"No Anton Gutman," Gum said.

I laughed. Anton is a bully in our sixth-grade class. None of us likes him much, but Gum thinks he's the absolute worst. The plane started to move toward the ground.

"Just a short bus ride to go," I said, "and we'll be at the Grand Canyon!"

* * *

Cat, Sam, Gum, and I grabbed the last row in the bus like we always do.

"I'm used to bus rides," Sam said, "but this is the nicest one we've ever had!"

We nodded. The bus was big and air-conditioned. The seats were plush and super comfortable. But most of all the scenery was amazing.

There were these cool rock formations, like huge rocks balancing on top of skinny rocks. There were bluffs of rock that looked like they'd been painted in long stripes, all different tones of orange.

"Getting some good shots, Edward?" Ms. Stanwyck asked. She's the Art Club faculty advisor, and our art teacher. She's probably the nicest teacher in school — and the shortest.

She stood in the aisle, holding on to the backs of the seats in front of the four of us.

"I sure am," I said. "The scenery does all the work to make these shots beautiful."

She smiled at me, and then she walked back toward the front of the bus. Right as she reached her seat, the bus slowed down. Then it rolled to a stop in a big parking lot.

We were finally there. Everyone climbed off the bus, chatting excitedly. Of course, with me, Gum, Sam, and Cat, we should have known this would be no ordinary field trip.

BURROS

The view from the rim of the canyon was totally mind-blowing.

I couldn't believe it! I knew the Grand Canyon was big, but wow! It went on for miles in every direction, and it was so deep!

"Okay, kids," Ms. Stanwyck said. "Get set up with your art projects and get started. We'll check into the motel after we break for lunch in one hour."

Cat got her easel set up on the rim of the canyon. Sam and Gum sat on a bench nearby and opened their big sketch pads. With my camera, I was able to move around a lot, so I walked along the rim.

Not far away, I saw a bunch of little hairy horses. They were corralled, and some men who looked like cowboys were standing nearby.

I took a few pictures. One of the men laughed and called out to me, "You like the burros?"

"Burros?" I said. "Is that what your little horses are called?"

He nodded. "They're not really horses," the man said. "Some visitors like to ride them down to the bottom of the canyon. It beats walking!"

Just then, a big man walked up with his wife and son. He seemed familiar to me, but I couldn't place it. I couldn't quite make out his son, either, since he was behind his parents.

The man who I'd been talking to went over to help the family. So I hurried back to my friend.

"Cat," I said, "you're not going to want to miss this."

"What?" Cat said. She was in the middle of her new painting and she didn't look up.

I held my camera's display in front of her so she could see a photo of a burro.

"Is that a pony?" she said. Her face lit up.

Cat loves every animal, from the slimiest slug to the most colorful bird and from the tiniest fish to the biggest lion.

I nodded. "Come on," I said. I led the way. Cat grabbed Sam's wrist, and then Gum had no choice but to follow too. He didn't want to sit there on the bench all by himself.

Cat ran ahead, pulling Sam with her.

"What's the big deal?" Gum said. He blew a bubble and let it pop. For a second, the air smelled of chocolate and peppermint.

"I found a bunch of burros," I said.

Gum gave me a confused look.

"They're like small horses," I said.

Gum nodded.

Up ahead, Cat and Sam were already at the burros. They had stopped a few feet off, afraid to get any closer. The big man who had arrived right after me was red in the face with anger. He was screaming at the man who ran the burro tours.

"We reserved three burros," he shouted, "and we want three burros."

The man running the tours didn't get flustered. I was impressed. I would have probably run off to hide. This big guy was scary. And he really was familiar. Still, I couldn't remember how I knew him.

Gum and I joined Cat and Sam a little closer to the burro's corral to listen in.

"I already told you, sir," the tour guide said. "You are too big for the burros. When you reserved, you said everyone in your party was under two hundred pounds."

I thought the big man would explode, he was so angry.

"I have never been so insulted!" he shouted. He took a deep breath and sucked in his belly. "I'm in the best shape of my life."

The tour guide took off his cowboy hat and scratched his head. "That may be, sir," he said. "But you're too big for my burros. I'm very sorry."

The big man's wife tried to calm him down, but it didn't help. Very quietly and carefully, I took a few pictures. The big man next to the burros was pretty funny, really. He made them seem even smaller. I could see why the guide wouldn't want him to sit on one.

"Then there's the issue of your grandson," the tour guide said. The grandson was standing behind his grandfather, so I couldn't see him.

"What about my grandson?" the big man said. "You're not about to tell me he is over two hundred pounds too?" He laughed.

"No," the guide said, "but he is too short. You said in your reservation that everyone in your family is over four feet and seven inches tall."

The big man was speechless now. He huffed and puffed, but he didn't say anything.

"Now, if your wife would like to take the tour by herself," the guide said.

"She would not," the big man said. Then he took her hand and dragged her off. "Let's go, honey." He shouted as he walked off, "Kid, I told you to wear your elevator shoes today!"

His grandson was still standing there near the corral, staring at the ground. He looked totally depressed by the whole thing. I couldn't tell if he was embarrassed, or sad to have disappointed his grandfather.

Maybe it was both.

Finally he lifted his head. My friends and I gasped. It was Anton Gutman!

"Anton!" Gum said. "What are you doing here?"

Anton sneered at us. "I'm here for a vacation with my grandparents," he said. "Obviously. What are you dorks doing here? I don't see a school bus anywhere, so this can't be a field trip."

"It is, actually," I said. "We took a plane, though."

"And a very fancy bus," Cat added. "It's our Art Club field trip."

"Ha-ha!" Anton said.
"More like Fart Club."

"Anton!" his grandfather snapped. He and his grandma had already walked pretty far off. "Come on!"

Anton was nearly in hysterics with laughter as he hurried off to catch up with his grandparents.

"What a jerk," Sam said. She punched her open hand with her fist. "Why, I oughta . . ."

"I can't believe he's here," Gum said. He shook his head. "And I thought this would be a normal field trip."

"For us?" I said. "It'll never happen."

"Hey, kids," the burro guide said. "Sorry to say, you won't be able to ride." He looked at Sam. "Well, you look tall enough, but your friends, I couldn't allow."

"That's okay," Sam said. "We're just here to enjoy the view."

"And photograph it," I added, holding up my camera.

"And paint it," Cat said. "Speaking of, we should get back to our stuff. We don't have much time till lunch."

The burro guide looked at his watch. "Ooh, you're right," he said. "It's just about time for me and the boys to shut down for lunch too. Have a good one!"

My friends and I went back to our art projects. We hardly got settled before we heard the burro guide yelling.

"Poncho!" he shouted. "Herbert! Louise! Where are you?"

Cat ran over to the burros' corral again. The three of us followed.

"What happened?" Cat asked.

The burros guide was in a panic. The other cowboys were running around, trying to calm the burros. "I don't understand it," the guide said. "The gate hasn't been open since this morning . . . I think."

"What happened, Mr. . . ." Sam asked.

The guide sighed. "Mr. Rito," he said. "And I can't find three of my burros."

"Oh no!" Cat said. She was obviously worried.

Mr. Rito nodded. He said, "They've been burro-napped!"

"Oh, those poor burros," Cat said. She was slumped on the bench near her easel. Gum and I patted her on the back and said things like, "There, there."

Sam paced in front of the bench, her hands behind her back, deep in thought. "Who would kidnap a little horse?" she muttered.

Gum rolled his eyes. "It's pretty obvious," he said.

Sam waved him off. "I know," she said. "You always think it's Anton. No matter what the crime, you think it's Anton."

"But it never is," Cat said. She sniffled and wiped her eyes with the back of her hand. She sure was upset about those burros.

"This time it is," Gum said. "And if it's not him, it's his father."

Cat sat up straight. "Hey, maybe Gum is right," she said, "for once."

Gum glared at her.

Cat continued. "His grandpa was obviously mad his family couldn't take a burro trip to the bottom of the canyon," Cat said. "And there were three of them: him, his wife, and Anton."

"And three burros went missing," Sam added. "I guess we better talk to Anton."

"Do we have to?" I said. "Anton and his goons have taken my camera from me and hidden it in garbage cans and bushes enough times, thanks."

Gum stood up and cracked his knuckles. "On this trip," he said, "Anton is without his goons. Let's find him."

It didn't take long. After a couple of minutes, we spotted Anton and his grandparents pushing their way to the front of the jeep tour line. I guess if they couldn't ride burros, they were going to find a spot on those jeeps.

The jeep tours were very popular. Everyone in line was holding their tickets already. I took a photo, then glanced at the line for the burros. It was empty. I guess most people who visit the Grand Canyon are just too heavy or too short for the burro tour.

"Um," Cat whispered to us. "Don't you have to reserve a space on those things like a year ahead of time?" She pointed at the Gutmans, who were arguing with the people at the front of the jeep line.

Sam nodded. "That's what I saw online," she said. "This ought to be interesting."

"Yeah," Gum said. "If a jeep or two goes missing next, I think we'll have our culprits for this trip."

That's when Mr. Gutman started to shout again. "I demand a spot on the next jeep to start out for the bottom of the canyon," he said.

Anton slinked away. Cat grabbed him by the arm. "We have to talk to you," she said in a kind voice. Cat is almost always nice to Anton — at least, she's more patient than the rest of us.

Then Sam got right in Anton's face. Her nose practically touched his and I think she snarled. "Where are those burros, Anton?" she said.

"Wh-what are you talking about?" Anton said. He leaned way back to put some space between himself and Sam. She's the tallest kid in sixth grade, which makes her about a foot taller than Anton — and me, for that matter. Luckily, she's my friend. Anton can't say the same.

"I'm talking about the missing burros, buddy," Sam said. "Your family's responsible. It's as plain as the nose on your face."

Gum blew a big bubble and let it pop. Anton jumped at the sound.

"I swear," Anton said, "I don't know anything about that!"

Sam put her fists on her hips and stared at Anton. "Don't leave town," she said. "We'll be watching you . . . and your grandparents, too."

Anton walked back toward his grandparents. "Don't leave town?" he mumbled. "Where would I go?"

Meanwhile, I'd taken a few photos of Mr. Gutman screaming at the jeep tour guide. Even after all that shouting, though, he was turned away without a spot on the tour. He and his wife, with Anton hurrying after, quickly left the scene.

"I'm going to write to my congressperson!" Mr. Gutman grumbled as they left. "This can't be legal."

"Okay, honey," his wife said. "Let's get you a snack."

Cat shook her head. "That is one angry man," she said.

"But is he angry enough to burro-nap?" Sam asked. She pulled out her little detective's pad and scribbled some notes. "We better follow them."

"Hey, you four," Ms. Stanwyck called out. She was with the rest of the Art Club at some picnic tables. "Come join us for lunch right away."

"I guess it'll have to wait," Gum said. He didn't look disappointed, though. Gum is never disappointed about lunchtime.

The four of us scored a great table with an amazing view. We all sat together on one side, happily chomping away at our sandwiches, gazing at the Grand Canyon.

I was thinking about how beautiful it was, and so different from where we live. And how big it was! It's crazy to think about, but the Grand Canyon is actually 277 miles long, and at some places almost 20 miles across. That means its volume is almost 3000 cubic miles. That is really, really big!

I glanced at Cat. She was smiling, chewing her cheese and cucumber sandwich. I knew she was probably marveling at the natural beauty of the canyon too.

I looked at Gum. His eyes were closed as he took a big bite of his huge hoagie. I think he was probably only thinking about that hoagie. Sam, of course, wasn't thinking about anything but the burro-nappers. She hardly touched her egg and onion sandwich.

"I guess they're our only suspects," Sam said. "If it's not the Gutmans, I'm stumped."

Gum nodded. "Me too," he said through a mouthful of bread and salami.

Just then, my view of the canyon was blocked — by Anton. He just sat down on the other side of the table from me and my friends and folded his hands.

"Hello, dorks," he said.

"What do you want, Anton?" Gum asked. "I'm trying to eat, and you're making me lose my appetite."

"I find that hard to believe," Anton said. He had a point.

"So what do you want?" I asked. Without his goons around, I felt a little braver standing up to him than I normally would have.

"Look, I know you all think my grandpa kidnapped those donkeys or whatever," Anton said. "But he didn't do it."

"Like you'd admit it," Sam said.

"I have another suspect for you," Anton said. "You probably haven't thought of this."

"Who?" I said.

"Someone who loves animals," Anton said.

We looked at each other, frowning.

Anton sighed, looking annoyed. Then he said, "Someone who would do anything to rescue animals from having to carry a bunch of fat old tourists all over the desert for hours at a time."

"Who?!" Gum demanded.

"Isn't it obvious?" Anton said. He looked right at Cat, and said, "It was Catalina Duran."

Cat jumped to her feet, nearly dropping half her sandwich. "What?!" she shouted. "How dare you!"

Anton laughed and got up from the table. He walked away casually with his hands up. "Relax," he said, laughing. "It's a free country, you know, and if you dorks can go around accusing my grandparents of burro-napping, I can suggest a better suspect."

Then, still laughing, he ran off.

"What a jerk," Cat said. She slumped in her seat and crossed her arms.

Sam put an arm around Cat. "Don't worry," she said. "We know you didn't do it."

"Yeah," Gum said, going back to eating his hoagie. "You have an air-tight alibi. You were with us!"

"Gum!" I said. "That's not why we know it wasn't Cat. We know because she's our friend and she would never do anything like this!" I glanced at Cat and Sam. "Right?" I said.

"Of course!" Cat snapped. I'd never seen her so upset.

For an instant, I wondered: Maybe she's a little *too* upset. But I chased the thought away and finished my lunch. Still, I noticed Sam carefully pull out her detective's pad and scribble something down.

Maybe she thought Cat
was a real suspect!

"Okay, Art Club members," Ms. Stanwyck said. "Let's clean up our lunches. Please don't leave any litter at your tables."

I grabbed my lunch box and my empty juice bottle. When Cat didn't move, I grabbed hers, too. "I'll get it," I said quietly. She just nodded and stared at her hands.

Sam and Gum hopped up with their empty paper bags and aluminum foil. They hurried over to the trash cans, threw out their garbage, and ran right over to their art projects.

"That's the spirit," Ms. Stanwyck said, watching them. "I'm glad to see you're so excited about your projects!"

I watched Gum and Sam talking. I couldn't hear what they were saying, but based on how sad Cat looked, I couldn't help thinking they were talking about her as a suspect.

"Let's get back to our projects," I said. I gave Cat a little nudge in the shoulder and smiled.

Cat stood up. "Okay," she said, but she still seemed down.

Slowly, we walked over to Cat's easel. I got a look at her painting. She'd done a great job showing how big the canyon is, and how deep. It was full of great shadows and colors.

"Hey, your painting looks great!" I said.

She mumbled, "Thanks." Then she grabbed a brush and started tapping at her color palette.

Sighing, I took the lens cap off my camera and started taking some shots. When I aimed toward the burros' corral, I noticed that one of them had slipped out of the open gate when the guide wasn't looking.

"Hey, Mr. Rito!" I called. He didn't hear me, so I grabbed my friends.

We hurried toward the corral. The escaped burro wasn't moving too fast, so we didn't have a hard time catching it.

"Hey there, burro," I said when we reached it. He kept walking.

Cat patted the burro on the neck. "Come back to your corral," she said quietly. It stopped, but it didn't head back home.

"I'll handle this," Gum said with a smirk. He grabbed the burro's rein and tried to guide it back toward the corral. It didn't budge.

"Whoa, there!" a big voice said. One of the cowboys jogged toward us. "Thanks for stopping old Mabel," he said.

"I saw her slip out," I said. "I tried to call, but I guess Mr. Rito didn't hear me."

The cowboy took the rein from Gum. "She won't go with just anyone," the cowboy said to Gum. "All the burros are faithful to Mr. Rito and us cowboys. They won't follow anyone else unless we say so." He laughed. "Of course, old Mabel here likes to wander over to the ice cream stand now and then," he said. "One of us cowboys — or Mr. Rito, of course — always has to come get her." Then he led her back to the corral.

Cat watched the old burro and the cowboy walk off. I snapped a photo. Then I glanced at Sam and Gum. They exchanged a glance, and I knew they were thinking about the burro-napping again.

Cat looked at her feet as she walked back to her easel.

OUTBURST

"Feeling pretty down, huh?" I said. I stood next to Cat's easel and looked through my camera at the canyon.

Cat shrugged. "I guess," she said.

"How come?" I asked.

Cat didn't answer. I heard the dry scrape of her brush on the canvas.

"It's because of the burro-napping, isn't it?" I asked. I clicked a photo.

Cat spun to face me, holding up her brush. A drop of paint landed on my shirt.

"Look, Egg," she snapped. I'd never seen so her agitated before. "I know what you're thinking. But I was not depressed about the overworked burros. I did not kidnap them so they wouldn't have to carry tourists anymore. So if you and Gum and Sam want to whisper about it, I don't care."

"I wasn't whispering to anyone!" I insisted.

"I didn't do it!" she said, practically shrieking. Then she went back to her painting. I decided not to risk trying to cheer her up anymore. Instead, I walked away, toward the burro corral.

As I left, I glanced at Sam and Gum. They had seen the whole outburst.

I knew Sam pretty well.

She was probably now
totally convinced that Cat
was the culprit.

Mr. Rito was leaning on the corral fence, watching the line for the jeep tours.

"Hi, Mr. Rito," I said as I walked up. "I met your burro Mabel earlier."

Mr. Rito tipped up his hat and looked at me. He said, "Thanks for keeping an eye on her when she slipped out."

"You still haven't found your missing burros, huh?" I asked.

Mr. Rito shook his head. Then he nodded toward the jeeps as they rumbled off to start another tour. "Look at that," he said. "Used to be the only way down was to walk or ride one of my burros."

"Not anymore," I said.

"You got that right," Mr. Rito said. "Now there are jeeps and helicopters. No one's interested in riding a burro nowadays."

"Business hasn't been good?" I asked.

Mr. Rito glared at me. "No," he said. "It hasn't." He spit on the ground. Then he turned and walked off toward the other cowboys.

"Edward Garrison!" Ms. Stanwyck called out.

I turned and waved to her. "I'm right here," I shouted.

"That's all for today," she called back. "Come on back, please."

I jogged over. "Now what are we doing?" I asked.

"Now," Ms. Stanwyck said, "we'll pack up, have some free time to look around and enjoy the gift shop, and then have supper and hit the hay."

"Sounds great," I said. I was tired.

I found my friends packing up their stuff near the edge of the canyon. Cat was still sulking. Gum and Egg stayed close together and hardly looked at her.

"Sorry about before," Cat said to me.

"It's okay," I said. "I don't think you're the one who did it."

She looked up and smiled at me.

"Thanks," she said.

I smiled back, and the two of us went to check out the gift shop. Gum and Sam didn't follow.

In the morning, Ms. Stanwyck gathered the Art Club members together in the motel lobby.

"Today, we'll take a short bus ride," she said. "We're going to see the Desert View Watchtower."

I glanced at my friends. None of us spoke. Gum and Sam were hunched close together, looking at her detective's pad. Cat didn't notice, or she pretended not to notice.

"The watchtower was designed by a famous architect named Mary Colter in the 1930s," Ms. Stanwyck explained.

Sam lifted her head. "A woman?" she said. "Cool."

Ms. Stanwyck smiled at her. "Yes," she said. "She designed the tower to resemble the traditional buildings of the Native Americans who lived in the area." She looked at me. "And Edward, the view from the top of the tower is said to be the best in the park. You'll get some great shots."

"Great," I said, trying to smile.

But my mind was still on the awkwardness among my friends.

* * *

Ms. Stanwyck was right about the tower.

I climbed all the way to the top, and the view was amazing. I snapped photo after photo. From the top, I could see all the way down to the bottom of the canyon.

Gum stayed at the top to sketch a little. Cat didn't have room to set up her easel, so she went back down with me. To my surprise, she set up her easel facing the tower, instead of the canyon.

"Um, the canyon is that way," I said.

"I know," Cat said. "But the tower is pretty cool-looking too."

She was right. It was seventy feet tall, according to Ms. Stanwyck, and made completely out of stones. Even though it was based on Native American buildings, to me it looked more like some old European castle. I snapped some photos of it.

Then Sam and Gum came out. They headed toward the gift shop.

"Um, I'm going to the gift shop," I told Cat. "I have to get something for my mom."

"Okay," she said without looking up.

I hoped she hadn't seen Gum and Sam go into the gift shop. I didn't want her to get the wrong idea again.

The shop was full of Native American arts and crafts. Gum and Sam weren't browsing. They were hunched over Sam's detective's pad again.

"What are you two up to?" I asked.

They both flinched. "Oh hi, Egg," Sam said. "We're just going over the clues for the mystery of the missing burros." She closed her pad and slipped it into her pocket.

"Can't I see?" I asked.

Sam glanced at Gum. "Um, there's nothing much to see," she said. "We're pretty sure it was Anton's grandpa."

"That's right," Gum said, nodding. "Anton's grandpa. Who else?"

"Then why don't we accuse him?" I asked. "Why don't we tell the police, or Mr. Rito?"

"Um," Gum said. "Because . . . we need better proof!"

"Then let's get it," I said. I stared at Sam.

"Right," Sam said. She forced a smile. "We'll get the proof as soon as we get back."

I squinted at her. "You're lying," I said.

"Am not!" they both said.

"You are," I insisted. "You both think Cat freed those burros, don't you?"

They both started talking at once. Sam said stuff like, "Of course we don't!" Gum said things like, "Well, it is possible. She loves animals!"

I sneered at them. Then I turned on my heels and stomped out of the gift shop.

When I reached Cat, she said, "No gift for your mom?" I didn't even stop. I just climbed onto the bus and sat in the last seat to wait for the drive back down toward our motel.

FRIENDS AGAIN

The bus pulled into the motel parking lot right around lunchtime. All the Art Club members were having a great time. Even Gum and Sam were acting like their normal selves.

Only Cat and I, slumped in the last seat on the bus, were sulking.

Once the bus stopped, Ms. Stanwyck came to the back to talk to us. She frowned. We frowned back. "Aren't you two enjoying the trip?" she asked.

We shrugged. "I guess," I said.

"Sure," Cat said.

Ms. Stanwyck thought for a moment. "Cat, I've really been impressed with your painting so far," she said.

"Thanks," Cat muttered.

Ms. Stanwyck looked at me. "Have you gotten some nice photos, Egg?" she asked. "I can't wait to see your prints, so we can display them in the art room!"

"That would be great," I said, faking a smile.

Ms. Stanwyck sighed. "Boy," she said, "you two are harder to move than those stubborn burros."

"What's that?" I said. Cat and I both perked up. "What about the burros?"

Ms. Stanwyck raised her eyebrows, but she went on. "I just mean Mr. Rito's burros," she said.

"Did you try to move them?" I said, wondering if we had a new suspect, finally.

"Me?" she said. "Of course not. But I saw Mr. Gutman — you know, Anton's grandfather — trying to move one this morning. It wouldn't budge!"

"Really," I said.

"Mmhm," said Ms. Stanwyck. "Finally one of those cowboys took the rein and told Mr. Gutman to bug off. He was too heavy to ride anyway." She shook her head. "I guess it takes a special person to lead one of those burros."

"Yeah," Cat said. "One of Mr. Rito's cowboys told us the same thing."

Ms. Stanwyck shrugged. "It's a shame about the three that got kidnapped," she said. "But I spoke to Mr. Rito this morning. He had them insured, so at least he won't go broke. Now, come on, kids."

Ms. Stanwyck turned and walked off the bus. Cat and I stared at each other.

"You thinking what I'm thinking?" I said.

Cat nodded.

"Let's go tell Sam," I said. I stood up and started for the door. Cat didn't follow. "Aren't you coming?" I said.

Cat looked at her hands. "You go," she said. "I don't really want to talk to Sam."

I rolled my eyes. Then I ran back and grabbed Cat's hand. "Come on," I said. "Let's just get it over with."

Gum and Sam were with the rest of the class. They had all gathered around the burros' corral, where Mr. Rito was slumped on a bench with his head in his hands.

"Another three burros are missing!" he wailed. A cowboy stood next to him, patting him on the shoulder.

"Hey, where have you two been?" Sam asked. She winked at Gum.

"Yeah," Gum said. "Has Egg been helping you free more burros, Cat?"

Cat didn't answer. She looked at her feet and her face turned red. But I wasn't going to keep quiet.

"I can't believe you two," I said. "After all the crimes we've solved together, you can't turn on Cat like this."

Sam frowned. "Well, what better suspect do we have?" she said. "Mr. Gutman?"

"He would be a better suspect than our best friend," I said. "But he's not the culprit either. The only possible suspects are Mr. Rito and his cowboys. After all, no one else can even move the burros, never mind kidnap them!"

Then I stomped over to Mr. Rito. "Isn't that right, Mr. Rito?" I said.

"What are you talking about, kid?" he asked.

Another cowboy stepped between me and Mr. Rito. "Leave him alone, kid," he said. "Can't you tell he's upset about the burros?"

I laughed. "The same way he's upset about the three burros that went missing yesterday?" I asked.

"Of course!" Mr. Rito said. "My business will fail without them."

Cat stepped up next to me. "It sounded to me like your business was failing anyway," she said. "Based on what you told Egg yesterday."

"Egg?" Mr. Rito repeated. "Who's Egg?"

"I am," I said. "And I also know that each of your burros is insured for enough to get you out of the burro-tour business without going broke."

Sam and Gum walked up then. "Business has been pretty bad?" Sam asked.

Mr. Rito looked at the crowd gathering around him. He laughed. "Well, I wouldn't say it's been bad," he said.

"But it's a lot worse than it used to be," I said. "Before they started the jeep tours and the helicopter tours."

"Is that right?" Sam said, smiling.

She turned to Cat. Cat didn't look her in the eyes.

"I'm sorry," Sam said. "I never should have suspected you."

Gum looked at Sam, and then at Cat, and then back at Sam. "Wait," he said. "What's going on?"

I poked him in the chest. "You believed Anton," I said, shaking my head. "Who would have thought?"

Cat laughed. "It's okay," she said. "I forgive them."

I smiled at her, and then at Sam and Gum. "Okay, then I do too," I said. Then I faced the cowboy. "Does Mr. Rito have a stable somewhere?" I asked.

"Of course," the cowboy said. "The burros don't sleep out here in the corral."

"Is there another stable?" I asked. "Maybe one he doesn't use a lot."

The cowboy took off his hat and scratched his head.

"Yes," he said. "It's down in the village. It was all boarded up the last time I was there. Mr. Rito told us to stay away."

Mr. Rito jumped to his feet. "And that's what I meant," he said.

"Ms. Stanwyck," Sam said. "Can you find a Park Ranger, please? I think they'll want to check out the stable down in the village."

"Yeah," I said. "I have a feeling they'll find six kidnapped burros in there, safe and sound."

Cat nodded. "They'll probably want to call Mr. Rito's insurance company, too," she said. "Because those six burros will be air-tight evidence of fraud if he's filed the claim."

Mr. Rito laughed nervously. He looked at his cowboy, who looked back with a quizzical squint.

"Is this true, Mr. Rito?" the cowboy asked.

Mr. Rito laughed again. "Of course not," he said. "Why, these kids . . ."

He didn't even finish, though. Instead he just started running, right down the sandy winding path to the bottom of the canyon.

The cowboy watched him go. "He won't get far like that," he said. "The rangers will catch him in their jeeps in no time."

We watched the rangers' jeeps barrel down the canyon road.

"Boy," I said, "Mr. Rito is really going to hate those jeeps now!"

Cat smiled. "Come on," she said. "I have a great idea for a new painting."

literary news

MYSTERIOUS WRITER REVEALED!

Steve Brezenoff lives in St. Paul, Minnesota, with his wife, Beth, their son, Sam, and their small, smelly dog, Harry. Besides writing books, he enjoys playing video games, riding his bicycle, and helping middle-school students work on their writing skills. Steve's ideas almost always come to him in his dreams, so he does his best writing in his pajamas.

arts & entertainment

ARTIST IS KEY TO SOLVING MYSTERY, SAY POLICE

Marcos Calo lives happily in A Coruña, Spain, with his wife, Patricia (who is also an illustrator), and their daughter, Claudia. When Marcos and Patricia aren't drawing, they like to go on long walks by the sea. They also watch a lot of films and eat Nutella sandwiches. Yum!

A Detective's Dictionary

alibi (AL-i-bye)—a claim that someone accused of committing a crime was somewhere else when the crime was committed

canyon (KAN-yuhn)—a deep, narrow valley with steep sides

corral (kuh-RAL)—a fenced area that holds horses, cattle

culprits (KUHL-prits)—the people who are guilty of doing something wrong or committing a crime

easel (EE-zuhl)—a folding wooden stand used to support a painting

evidence (EV-uh-duhnss)—information and facts that help prove something

fraud (FRAWD)—cheat or trick

obvious (OB-vee-uhss)—easy to see or understand

reservation (rez-ur-VAY-shuhn)—an arrangement to save space or a seat

tourists (TOOR-ists)—people who travel and visit places for pleasure

volume (VOL-yoom)—the amount of space in an area

Edward G. Garrison

Sixth Grade

(A)

The Grand Canyon

The Grand Canyon is located in Grand Canyon National Park in Arizona. It is 277 miles long, 18 miles wide in some spots, and more than a mile deep in some spots.

The Grand Canyon was created by the Colorado River over the course of about 17 million years, according to scientists. The river slowly eroded the land, creating a huge canyon. The river still runs through the canyon.

In 1908, the Grand Canyon became a national landmark, and it became a national park in 1919.

The Ancient Pueblo People were the first humans to live in the area. Archaeologists think they settled there around 1200 B.C. Since then, the area has been continually settled by Native Americans.

Many artists have been inspired by the natural beauty of the canyon. Every year, artists are chosen for the Grand Canyon Artists-in-Residence program. Art inspired by the canyon is also displayed in many area galleries and around the United States.

Edward, fabulous! I hope our class can return to the Grand Canyon again soon to be inspired by it again!

– Ms. S.

FURTHER INVESTIGATIONS

CASE #FTMEGGENP15

1. In this book, my class went on a field trip. What field trips have you gone on? Which one was your favorite, and why?

2. If you went on a field trip to the Everglades, what would you be most excited to see? Talk about your answer.

3. Who else could have been a suspect in this mystery?

IN YOUR OWN DETECTIVE'S NOTEBOOK . . .

1. Write about a time you couldn't trust an adult. What happened?

2. Sam, Cat, Gum, and Egg are best friends. Write about your best friend.

3. This book is a mystery story. Write your own mystery story!

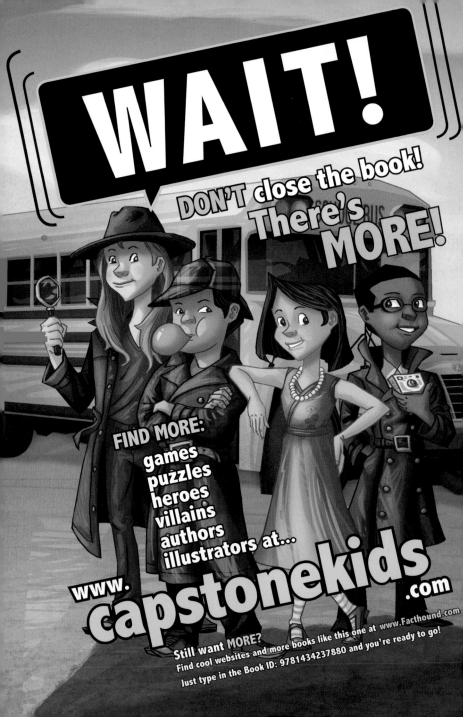